Mai's
Lesson

by Elizabeth Nielsen
illustrated by Ki-Hun Yu

a Capstone company — publishers for children

Engage Literacy is published in the UK by Raintree.
Raintree is an imprint of Capstone Global Library Limited, a company incorporated in England and Wales
having its registered office at 264 Banbury Road, Oxford, OX2 7DY – Registered company number:
6695582

www.raintree.co.uk

Editorial credits
Marissa Kirkman, editor; Steve Mead, designer; Katy LaVigne, production specialist

Illustrated by Ki-Hun Yu - Advocate Art

21 20 19 18
10 9 8 7 6 5 4 3 2 1
Printed and bound in India.

Mai's Lesson

ISBN: 978 1 4747 4700 4

Contents

Chapter 1
The jade flute. 4

Chapter 2
The first lesson 8

Chapter 3
Lost!. 14

Chapter 4
Master Sheng's message 18

Chapter 5
The big day 26

Chapter 1

The jade flute

Mai opened her eyes and saw a soft pink glow in the morning sky. Her heart soared. The day of her first flute lesson had finally arrived! To calm the butterflies in her stomach, she reached into her sleeve and rubbed the jade flute, or xiao, that was hidden inside. It was too important a treasure to sleep with like a toy, but she could not bear to part with it. It had belonged to her mother, and touching it was almost like holding her mother's hand. Almost. It had been three years since she had lost her parents, and Mai still missed them every day.

"I'll make you proud, Mother," she whispered. "One day, I'll be famous across all of China."

It was a big promise, but Mai felt that her flute made it possible. After all, it was a very special flute. Most flutes were made of bamboo. But hers was carved out of green jade stone. It had been in her mother's family for many years. According to an old family story, an ancient ruler had given it to an ancestor with a gift for music. Some even said it had magical powers.

Like her mother, Mai's talent was amazing. At only nine years old, she had been invited by the Emperor to take lessons and perform before his court. And today she would start! Mai jumped from her bed, hugging the treasured flute. She couldn't wait to take the first step towards reaching her dream.

Just then there was a soft knock on the door. The Emperor's wife entered the room. She smiled when she saw the jade flute. "Just as I thought. When I found your treasure missing from its case this morning, I had a feeling I'd find it here. Did you sleep well?"

"Yes, Auntie, thank you," said Mai shyly. Calling such a grand lady, Auntie, still seemed strange to Mai. But it was what the Empress had asked. Mai's father had been the Emperor's cousin. The Empress always made sure Mai and her older brother, Hung, felt at home in the palace.

"I just wanted to wish you a wonderful first day of lessons, Mai," said the Empress kindly. "The Emperor and I are certain you will bring great honour to our family."

Chapter 2

The first lesson

Mai skipped ahead of Hung on their way to the royal music school. The flute players were one of several groups within the Emperor's band of musicians. Every week, the entire band came together to play for the Emperor in his famous pear garden. "Hung! Can you believe that soon I'll be playing for the Emperor? Oh, wouldn't Mother be excited?"

"She certainly would," said Hung, smiling. They had reached the flute players' practice room, and it was time to say goodbye. "Can you find your way back?" he asked. He knew that Mai sometimes got lost in the huge palace.

"I'll be fine," said Mai. "You must get to the stables to feed Ling Ling." Ling Ling was the Emperor's panda. The Emperor had honoured Hung with the special job of being Ling Ling's caretaker.

Just then, two older girls carrying bamboo flutes arrived. They stared at Mai for a moment before entering the room. "She's so young!" Mai heard one whisper. "She's only here because her father was the Emperor's cousin," the other replied.

The sparkle in Mai's brown eyes faded. *Could that be true?*

"Don't worry," said Hung. "Listen closely to Master Sheng, and you'll prove that you're worthy of playing for the Emperor."

Mai took a deep breath and stepped inside. About ten students sat on mats, facing a tall man with a long beard. Master Sheng! Mai found a small mat and spread it on the floor.

After a long silence, the master began to play. One by one, the other students joined him. But the song was more difficult than any Mai had ever learned. She glanced around nervously. Everyone seemed to be at least four years older. And all had bamboo flutes.

When the song ended, Mai found Master Sheng's gaze upon her. "Songs," he said, "are stories without words. What story do you think that song tells, Mai?"

"I . . . I . . . don't know, Master Sheng," Mai said shyly. Her cheeks burned bright red. Someone giggled.

"Ji!" said Master Sheng, looking hard at a player to Mai's right. It was one of the girls from the doorway.

"I'm sorry, Master Sheng," the girl said, bowing her head.

Master Sheng turned his stiff gaze back to Mai. "Before one can be a great storyteller, one must be a great listener. Now, child, tell us a story that you know."

Her heart was pounding. Mai raised her flute to her lips and began to play a tune her mother taught her. It reminded her of the wind blowing softly on a pond. But her breath was shaky, and her fingers slipped on the pipe. The sound came out all wrong. She felt everyone staring at her. They could only be thinking one thing. *You don't belong here!*

Mother would have been so ashamed! It was more than Mai could bear. She had to escape! Blinded by tears, she stumbled to the door and ran.

Chapter 3

Lost!

"Mai!" cried Hung, racing into the garden. "I've been looking everywhere for you! What happened?"

Mai looked up from where she was hiding, her eyes red. "Oh, Hung. It was terrible. They think I don't belong there. After the way I played today, they may be right."

"Who is, they? Who thinks you don't belong there?" asked Hung.

"That girl at the doorway. Probably everyone else, too."

"You don't know that. Don't give up on your dream so easily. You can try again tomorrow. Come on, let's go home."

Mai let Hung pull her to her feet. "Thank you, Hung. I feel a little bit better." But as she reached inside her sleeve, her eyes widened in fear. "Hung!" she cried. "My flute is missing! Oh, what will Auntie say?"

Mai and Hung searched all over the garden, but the flute was nowhere to be found. Seeing that Mai was becoming upset, Hung spoke calmly. "Did you have it when you left the lesson? Which way did you take to get here?"

"I don't know! All I could think about was running away!"

"Don't worry," said Hung. "We'll find your flute. Maybe it fell out of your sleeve, or maybe you left it behind. Either way, I know it will turn up."

But it didn't.

Mai and Hung looked everywhere, but the jade flute had vanished. Mai was heartbroken. It was like losing her mother all over again. And it was all her fault!

That night, she had a terrible dream. Her mother looked on sadly as the entire music school pointed at Mai. They cried, "You don't belong here!"

When sunlight crept across her face the next morning, Mai pulled the blanket over her head. Hung knocked firmly on the door. "Come on, Mai," he called. "Time for your lesson."

"I'm not going to my lesson! I have no flute, remember?"

"You can borrow one from Master Sheng. Now let's go. Remember what Mother used to say: 'No one ever reached the top of a mountain by wishing.' Time to climb, Mai."

Chapter 4

Master Sheng's message

An hour later, Mai was seated again on the small mat. This time, she held a simple bamboo flute borrowed from Master Sheng. Like the jade flute, it had five holes on top and one below. It too was beautifully made. But it felt like a stranger.

When Master Sheng began playing, Mai was pleased to hear a familiar tune. She brought the bamboo flute to her lips and began to play.

CHIRRRP! CHIRRRP!

Mai paused, confused. Had that choppy, ugly sound come from her? Maybe she had just been too forceful with her breath. She tried again, but it was no use. Her music was like that of a newborn sparrow, not a full-grown songbird.

"I see the truth now," she thought sadly. "It was the jade flute, not me, that made such beautiful music. Without it, I am nothing."

When the song was over, she rolled up the small mat and bowed to Master Sheng. Then she walked to the door. Her dream was over. She heard Ji whisper, "See? It takes more than a fancy flute."

Mai knew she was right.

That night, Mai and Hung went to the palace stables to visit Ling Ling. Heartbroken, Mai buried her face in the panda's soft fur. Hung squeezed her shoulder but said nothing. His attempts to convince her not to quit had failed.

Suddenly, firm footsteps announced that someone was coming. It was Master Sheng! Mai stood up quickly and wiped her eyes.

"Ah, I thought I'd find you here," said Master Sheng with a kind smile. "Ling Ling understands how to comfort a troubled heart." He looked at the three of them fondly. "Now, I must ask you to walk with me, Mai. There is something you must know."

"Of course, Master Sheng," said Mai. She bowed her small head and fell into step beside him.

21

"A long time ago," said Master Sheng, "I had the honour of teaching your mother. As you know, she became a very great musician. Perhaps the best in her family. But what you may not know is that it took a very, very long time. Her talent did not come as easily as many before her. She just worked much, much harder."

Mai looked at him in wonder. It was hard to believe that her amazing mother had ever struggled.

Master Sheng nodded. "And now I must say goodnight. But I would like to leave you with one final thought. There is indeed magic in the music, Mai. But it does not come from the flute."

After awhile, Mai rejoined Hung and Ling Ling. The sparkle had returned to her eyes. "No more turning back," she promised. "From now on, I will climb until I reach the mountain top!"

Mai was true to her word. Every day, she sat on her small mat and worked hard. Master Sheng said that a new flute was like a new friend. You had to get to know one another before you could share secrets. Slowly, Mai got to know the bamboo flute. Its music began to sound more like the smooth silk that had once flowed from her jade one. Perhaps even better.

Meanwhile, Mai began to gain the respect of the other students. She heard no more giggling from Ji, and no one seemed to judge her when she played.

On the day before the class was to play for the Emperor, Master Sheng gave an announcement. Mai would be given a solo. "It is the Emperor's wish, which you have earned."

Mai stood and bowed. "Thank you, Master Sheng. I am honoured. However, I would prefer to be one bird among many in the dawn."

"What do you mean?" asked Master Sheng.

"I've been thinking about that song you played at my first lesson. I know now what story it tells. It is the story of the world waking up. Each flute is the voice of a different songbird greeting the day. I wish to be but one small voice among you all, celebrating."

"Very well," said Master Sheng. "I shall speak to the Emperor."

Chapter 5

The big day

The next morning, Mai dressed in her best pink robe. Then she closed her eyes and made a wish.

Suddenly, she heard a soft knock on the door. The Empress came in, smiling.

"You remind me more of your mother every day, Mai. She would be so proud of how hard you have worked. I know I am." And then the Empress drew from the sleeve of her golden robe . . . the jade flute!

Mai was amazed. "How did you . . . I was afraid to tell you . . . "

The Empress smiled. "Master Sheng brought this to me after you dropped it. We agreed that you had to learn some things before you were ready to play it again."

"About music?" asked Mai.

"No, Mai, about yourself." The Empress held out the flute. "About what being a great player means. I think you have earned the right to this magnificent flute now."

Deeply touched, Mai bowed her head and took the flute. "Thank you, Auntie," she said. "Thank you for the flute – and the lesson." Calling the most powerful woman in China, Auntie, suddenly felt just right.

Later, Mai walked with the rest of the flute players to the pear garden. She and Master Sheng had shared only a brief glance, but it had been enough. When he saw what she was carrying, the wise teacher had smiled and nodded.

The flute players took their places among the rest of the court musicians and waited for the Emperor to arrive. Mai could hardly believe she was standing there among them.

At last, the Emperor took his place at the centre. He signalled to a servant, who brought him a drum. The Emperor was going to perform with them!

At the Emperor's nod, Master Sheng began to play. The slow, sweet sound became the first voice of the new day. After a few moments, Mai raised her flute and joined him in a playful duet. They were two songbirds, wishing each other good morning. She saw the Emperor beam with pleasure. Then Ji flew in. Their eyes met, and Mai was surprised to see Ji bow slightly in her direction.

Perhaps one day she and Ji might become friends.

For now, Mai, Ji and Master Sheng were three soaring voices among many. Even the Emperor had joined the band of instruments. He was beating his drum faster and faster as the sun rose higher and higher in the sky. The Empress smiled proudly.

Mai's heart swelled with pride. It was better than fame.

As she played her mother's jade flute, Mai felt her past and present join. Together they made something that was simply magical.